P9-DIJ-312

THE TRUTH ABOUT MY UNBELIEVABLE SUMMER...

THE TRUTH ABOUT MY UNBELIEVABLE SUMMER...

For Sibilla and Morgana
—Davide

For Jules

—Benjamin

ISBN 978-1-338-09590-6

12 11 10 9 8 7 6 5 4 3 2 1   16 17 18 19 20 21

Printed in the U.S.A.   40

First Scholastic printing, September 2016

Design by Ryan Hayes
Typeset in 1820 Modern

THE TRUTH ABOUT MY UNBELIEVABLE SUMMER...

Davide Cali   Benjamin Chaud

SCHOLASTIC INC.

Well, you may not believe this, but ...

I found a message in a bottle. It wasn't just
any message—it was a treasure map!

Then a magpie pecked it out of my hands!

So I chased the bird all the way onto a ship in port.

Apparently, the crew didn't appreciate unexpected guests.

Just when I thought I'd escaped,
I almost became a giant squid's lunch.

Luckily, I was rescued by a submarine captain . . .

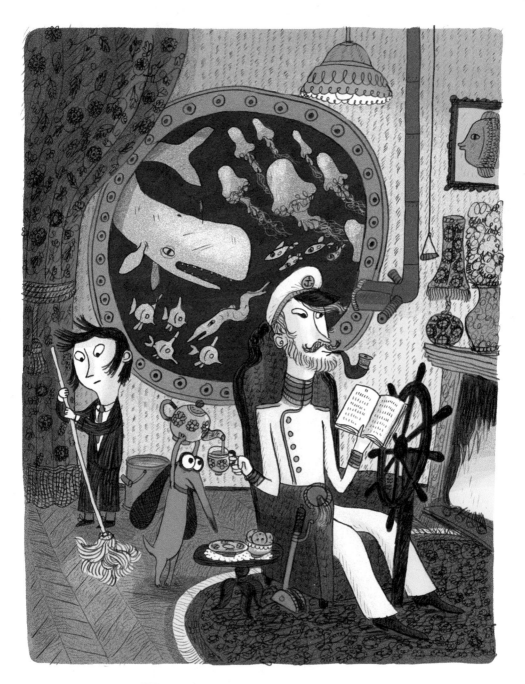

Who promptly put me to work.

When the submarine finally surfaced,
we had traveled back in time!

"How did *that* happen?"

It didn't. Actually, it was just some
people making a movie.

Then, by chance, I met an actress who
knew exactly where to find my map!

It was just a little out of reach . . .

Anyway, the treasure hunt was back on!

But something went wrong . . .

And I ended up in the desert.

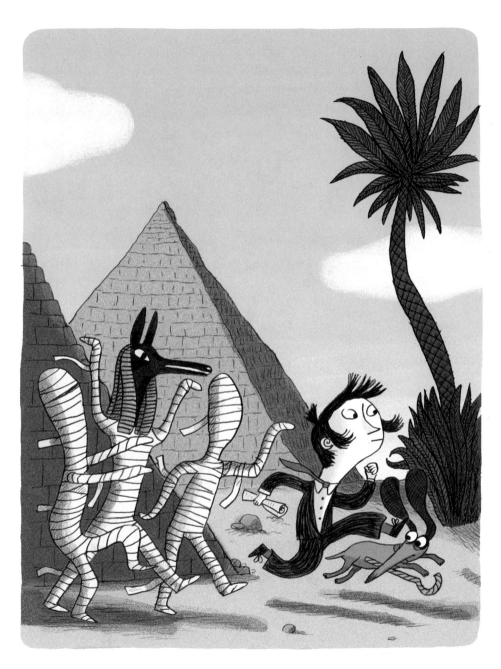

It turns out that my arrival disturbed some deep sleepers.

At just the right moment,
my uncle passed by in his latest invention.

Since it was still experimental, there were some surprises.

My uncle dropped me off on
a deserted island, where the
magpie stole my map *again*.

"Was it really the same bird?"

Yes! I have no idea how it found me!

I chased that bird everywhere.

And I mean, *everywhere*.

At last, I had it!

So I hitched a ride down the mountain.

And then I remembered my uncle's jet pack!

Once airborne, it was easy to follow the map's directions.
X marked the spot . . .

Back where I started! And I couldn't believe it . . .

This was the treasure?!

Still, I guess my summer was OK.

So you probably don't believe me . . . right?

Three months earlier . . .

- The End -

Davide Cali is an author, illustrator, and cartoonist who has published more than 40 books, including *I Didn't Do My Homework Because . . .*, *A Funny Thing Happened on the Way to School . . .*, and *I Didn't Do My Homework Because Doodle Book of Excuses*. He lives in France and Italy.

Benjamin Chaud has illustrated more than 60 books. He is the illustrator of *I Didn't Do My Homework Because . . .*, *A Funny Thing Happened on the Way to School . . .*, and *I Didn't Do My Homework Because Doodle Book of Excuses*. He is the author and illustrator of New York Times Notable Book *The Bear's Song*, *The Bear's Sea Escape*, *The Bear's Surprise*, and *Farewell Floppy*, as well as the Pomelo series. He lives in Die, France.